This book is attributed to:

David, Jill and Anna-Marie
without whom this book could
not have been written. Thank
you for all the inspiration,
support and encouragement you
have shown.

Contents:

Introduction

Dangerous Dave really wasn't that dangerous! In fact I am not sure that Dangerous Dave ever did ANYTHING that was particularly dangerous.

No... Dangerous Dave was like a grandad who ended up getting caught up in trouble at times

It's not that he wasn't thinking...no, it's just that perhaps he wasn't thinking in the right direction... that perhaps his thoughts had gone off to visit some other place just for a little while before making a speedy return back to earth!

I am immensely fond of Dangerous Dave, not just because of his adventures and calamities; but simply because he is one of my own family.

I hope you thoroughly enjoy these amusing (and true!) stories.

Chapter 1

Dangerous Dave and the Car

For years and years Dangerous Dave had not been able to drive. This hadn't been a problem for him as he was quite used to walking to all the places he needed to go providing he didn't feel too tired as there were too large hills on his street – one to the left; and one to the right.

So most mornings, Dangerous Dave would leave his little house, turn left and walk down the little hill to the shop where he worked.

The little shop sold carpentry and engineering tools; and

Dangerous Dave knew lots about tools. What he couldn't do though was use them. When his wife, Daphne, would ask him to fix something with his tools, she would normally end up asking someone else to come and repair what Dangerous Dave had supposedly fixed.

Dangerous Dave would spend his time at the shop talking to his customers, making cups of coffee and tea, playing a game of darts in the backroom and occasionally selling some of his tools.

The problem would come when a customer popped in to ask Dangerous Dave if he could come to their house to buy some tools.

This was a problem! The only solution was to talk to Daphne very nicely and see if she would be kind enough to drive him out to see more tools. Daphne was not too keen to do this job. First it meant that she couldn't do the housework, the cleaning or looking after their two children, Will and Sarah.

But even worse than that was the fact that Dangerous Dave's sense of direction was not always right. 'Turn left,' he would shout after just going past the turning; and the little Renault car would come to a sudden halt, reverse back down the road and then start down the next little lane.

So many times they would end up in the wrong place. Dangerous Dave would rub his forehead, look left and right out the windows, look at the map and then say 'We're not where I thought we would be' which was even more annoying for Daphne who was driving the car. Eventually though they would get there. Dangerous Dave would look at the tools with lots of thoughts about money and becoming rich going through his brain; whilst Daphne would sit there with lots of thoughts about dirt, rust and old plastic boxes full of tools – and how the car would need a clean later that day.

This routine went on for days, weeks, months and years...until one day, Dangerous Dave had an idea!

'I know,' he said. 'I am going to learn to drive!'

'You going to do what?' said Daphne.

'I'm going to learn to drive,' said Dangerous Dave. 'Then I can go wherever I want. You wouldn't need to come and get the tools. I could go by myself'.

'Are you sure this is a good idea?' asked Daphne.

'What happens if you get lost?' said Will.

'And even worse, what happens if you crash?'

But Dangerous Dave had made up his mind! He was going to learn to drive. His family were most concerned and pointed out to him some of the dangers of driving; but when Dangerous Dave had made his mind up about something, no-one was going to change it!

So Dangerous Dave chose a driving instructor to teach him how to drive. His family thought the driving instructor was very brave! They watched out the window as the learner car would start and then bunny-hop along the street, looking as if it were almost choking on the petrol it was drinking.

At the road junction the little car would stop, then jerk forward, stop again, jerk forward again, screech a little whilst the gears were being changed and then eventually crawl along the road with its normal choking sound.

As time went on however, the driving got a little better. The car had stopped bunny hopping and now Dangerous Dave just had to be reminded of a few other things.

'Get back on the left side of the white line.'

'Breeeaaaaakkkk!'

'Mind the cyclist'.

'Slow down, you're going too fast.'

After lots of lessons, lots of tellings-off from the driving instructor and lots of failed tests, Dangerous Dave finally passed his test! He was so excited! Daphne was really scared as they would now need to share the car and she didn't want to see it broken.

Dangerous Dave would now be able to go and buy tools for himself. An agreement was made that Dangerous Dave could have the car at the weekends; when Daphne didn't need to take Will and Sarah to school. They would simply walk to the local library, the play park or the shopping on a Saturday and then go to the Baptist Church on a Sunday.

One Sunday, Dangerous Dave, Daphne, Will and Sarah were invited to go to their friends, Stan and Val, for Sunday lunch. They didn't live too far away, which was a good thing because Dangerous Dave was driving!

'Can Mum drive please?' said Will, really worried that Dangerous Dave might crash the car.

'No,' said Dangerous Dave. 'I am quite capable of driving the car.'

'Mum... please can you drive?' Will tried again.

'No, dear,' came the reply. 'Your dad is going to drive.'

'Oh no!' cried Will.

'It will be fine,' said Dangerous Dave. 'I do know what I am doing.'

And so off they set, slowly at first, with the little Renault doing its usual choking sounds to start with, over-revving of the engine later before finely making the sound of a normal car engine happily going round and round.

'Stop, stop,' cried Will as they got near the junction. The car came to a sudden halt.

'I know about the junction,' said Dangerous Dave, just missing the cyclist going by.

And off they would go again.

'Careful, careful...' said Daphne as Dangerous Dave took the car up on the kerb whilst turning onto the main road.

'Someone's crossing over' screamed Will as the car went whizzing over the zebra crossing; but Dangerous Dave was more than happy behind the steering wheel. That was until the next junction...

It was a simple turning – just a right turn from the main road into the small street where Stan and Val lived, just a few houses away. On the corner was a fairly large house with a big wooden fence going around the side garden and next to that was the lamppost.

'You've gone a bit far to make a good turn,' said Daphne.

'No, I can do it,' said Dangerous Dave.

'Really?' said Will from the backseat. 'Wouldn't it be better to let mum drive?'

'No!' said Dangerous Dave, becoming most annoyed. 'I do know how to drive!' And with that he started to turn the wheel and move off in the direction of the street.

Whether Dangerous Dave hadn't seen the lamppost, the wooden fence or indeed the road name still remains a mystery; but as the little Renault suddenly took off, things all happened very quickly.

The little car went too fast and narrowly missed the lamppost, the road name and just avoided taking the man's wooden fence down altogether.

'Aaaaaaah', screamed Will from the backseat.

'Stop!' cried Daphne from the front seat.

'It's alright,' said Dangerous Dave. 'The car just went faster than I told it to'. He hit his hand on the steering wheel to tell the car off for its bad behaviour.

Three houses further up the road, Dangerous Dave smiles and

says 'See, I got you here safely.'
Daphne, Will and Sarah all got
out, their hearts still beating
wildly.

'Please can mum drive home,'
moaned Will.

Things did improve over time
however and remarkably
Dangerous Dave had dreams of
becoming a taxi driver as he said
he knew all the roads really well.
He could still collect tools as a
hobby!

One day however, Dangerous
Dave took his family to Weyford
where there was a big shopping
centre to look round, full of
exciting things like tools,
antiques, and more tools, and

other old things. He was very excited and very keen to go.

So that morning Dangerous Dave was up early. He made himself his black coffee and breakfast (usually biscuits!) before getting washed and then putting on his working clothes, ready to go and see tools and the other exciting things.

Daphne and the children took a little more time and after having had a sensible breakfast, got themselves looking fairly smart and announced that they were ready to go.

Dangerous Dave was already in the car, waiting to leave. Daphne,

Will and Sarah got in and off they went to Weyford.

It took about forty five minutes to get there and whilst they went, Will and Sarah would play 'Car Cricket' in the back seat in which they would have to spot different colour cars for a bowl or a bat and keep scores of who was winning. It was Will's favourite car game and was usually accompanied by Dangerous Dave's whistling or singing – sometimes with the correct words.

The car park at Weyford was tricky because it was all uphill with the shopping centre being at the bottom. Dangerous Dave pulled into the car park. So far the journey had been a real success and no close accidents had taken place.

The only space available was near the top of the hill in which the car would have to pull in behind another car facing downhill. Dangerous Dave considered that this space would be most suitable despite the fact that he and his family would have to walk all the way to the top of the hill with their shopping later that afternoon.

Dangerous Dave successfully pulled the little Renault into the space between two other parked cars and safely put the brake on before hitting the car in front of him. Daphne, Will and Sarah sighed a big sigh of relief.

'You go to the shopping centre,' said Dangerous Dave to Daphne and the children. 'I will meet you just inside after I have bought the parking ticket'. And that's just what they did.

Daphne, Will and Sarah were waiting quite a long time inside for Dangerous Dave to appear; and when he did, his face was all white as if he had seen a ghost.

'Are you alright?' asked Daphne, noticing that Dangerous Dave was shaking a little.

'What's happened, Dad?' asked Will.

'I've just hit three cars,' said Dangerous Dave with a quiver in his voice.

'You were only buying a parking ticket', replied Daphne. 'How did you do that?'

'Well,' said Dangerous Dave. 'It was like this...' and he proceeded to tell the story. 'When I came back from the ticket machine, the car in front of us had gone and there was an empty space and I thought to myself that it would be easier to get out of the car park later on if I drove out of the front space forward than to reverse out of the space we were in'.

'Go on,' said Daphne curiously.

'Well,' said Dangerous Dave. 'I got in the car and let go of the handbrake so the car could roll into the space in front.'

'Did you turn the car on?' said Will, fascinated by the story so far.

'Well, that was the problem,' replied Dangerous Dave. 'When the car started to roll, the steering was locked and I couldn't move it. So I hit the car next to me. Then I panicked so I quickly turned the car on and swung the steering wheel the other way and that's when I hit the second car.'

'I am beginning to see what happened so far,' said Daphne,

looking quite irritated, 'but how did you hit the third car?'

'Well,' said Dangerous Dave, looking quite forlorn by now, 'when I hit the second car, I forgot what I was doing and by then the car had started rolling faster and faster and that's when I hit the next car in front – in the next row of cars!'

Daphne was not very pleased at all. She went to look at the car, which amazingly enough had survived all of its bumps with very little scratches or dents. Dangerous Dave tried to look away as the cars around now had nice new stripes in their paintwork or little dents in their doors and bumpers.

'Still, it wasn't really my fault,' said Dangerous Dave. 'Shall we go and enjoy ourselves now?'

Chapter 2

Dangerous Dave and the Water

If there was one thing that Dangerous Dave was not keen on, it was water. Washing up the dishes was fine because that only involved his hands going into the water; paddling in the sea was also okay because that only meant putting his feet into the water; washing his face before and after bedtime was also acceptable because that didn't involve too much water either; but anything more than that was considered dangerous!

How this avoidance of water started, no-one was quite sure.

He had always seemed happy to do the washing up, water the garden, occasionally wash the car and usually the cat at the same time! But at some point in his history Dangerous Dave clearly had had a bad experience with water!

It had something to do with Dangerous Dave being in control of the water. If he was controlling the water then maybe all was okay and over time, Dangerous Dave managed to conquer the idea of having a bath! The water could be run until it was exactly the right temperature – something he would always test with his elbow and fingers before putting a foot anywhere near the edge of the bath. Then he could slowly and gradually slip into the bath without getting too much of him wet at one time. Sat in the half-filled bath of water he could then keep an eye on what all the little waves and soapy suds were up to. Any problems with the water could easily be put right by simply pulling the plug out!

One day, Dangerous Dave was out with Will and Sarah and some friends they also had invited. The children decided that they wanted to go swimming. Dangerous Dave didn't like this idea very much at all.

'Do you want to go ice-skating?' he said

'No, we want to go swimming!' cried the children.

'We could go to Pauline's Play Park' suggested Dangerous Dave.

'We want to go swimming,' said Will and Sarah. All their friends joined in too. 'Swimming, swimming, swimming...' they chanted.

Dangerous Dave grunted, got everyone in the car and drove to Bourneville Swimming Centre.

Now Bourneville Swimming Centre was a very exciting place to go. It had two pools, a large water slide, a wave machine and inflatable toys. The lifeguards were also very friendly and you could play 'hide and seek' – that was until they blew the whistle if you stayed under the water for too long – just in case you were drowning.

Dangerous Dave, Will, Sarah and their friends all arrived and hurriedly rushed off to the changing rooms.

'Come on, dad' said Will. 'The girls will already be in there – hurry up.'

'I'm coming as quickly as I can' said Dangerous Dave, but you could tell he wasn't being very quick at all.

Will, Sarah and their friends were having a great time in the pool. They splashed water over each other, had swimming races to see who could get to the other side first, played underwater chase, jumped up and down in the waves of the wave machine, and went for hundreds of rides down the water slide.

After nearly an hour a little grey head appeared poking round the side of the changing room entrance. It was Dangerous Dave. He was looking very nervous, glancing left and right – almost as if to see if anybody was going to notice him.

'What's he doing?' said Will.

'Has he only just finished changing into his swimming trunks? It's been nearly an hour I think.'

'I wonder if he's okay,' said Will, concerned.

'He's fine,' said Sarah dismissingly. 'He's probably still scared of going near the water'.

As the words finished coming out of her mouth, Dangerous Dave did a sudden sprint like movement from the changing room entrance to the poolside. Will and Sarah had never in their whole lives seen their dad move so quickly into the water!

'Wow!' said Will. 'He really is keen to get into water after all.'

'I'm not so convinced,' said Sarah. 'Let's go and see if he's okay'.

By now Dangerous Dave had got the water nearly up to his waist, which amazed Will, Sarah and their friends even more.

'How are you finding the water, dad?' said Will.

'It's a bit cold,' said Dangerous Dave. 'But don't ask me to swim because I don't know how.'

'We could teach you,' suggested Sarah.

'No,...no,...I don't think so,' replied Dangerous Dave. 'I think I would rather keep my feet on the floor. I will just walk up and down in the pool. You go and have fun!'

And for the next ten minutes that's what happened. Will, Sarah and their friends continued to play and enjoy themselves – that was until there was a long whistle from the lifeguard.

Everyone in the pool paused to see what the lifeguard was whistling about.

'You,' he said, pointing to Dangerous Dave. 'Out of the pool now'.

Dangerous Dave's face turned red. He felt extremely embarrassed. He didn't like swimming pools and now everyone was looking at him as if he was a criminal of some sort.

'What's he done?' said Sarah.

'I don't know,' said Will. 'But don't worry – they probably don't want him to walk up and down in the swimming lanes. Perhaps he's got in the way of the swimmers or something. Now come on, it's my turn to go down the water slide'.

'Okay,' replied Sarah.

She followed Will off to the water slide.

The lifeguard, in the meantime, had left his special seat and was walking to the edge of the shallow end of the pool to meet Dangerous Dave.

'Excuse me, sir,' said the lifeguard. 'What's your name?'

'Dave,' replied Dangerous Dave. 'They call me Dangerous Dave'.

'Oh, dangerous, are we?' said the lifeguard.

'Not really,' replied Dangerous Dave.

'Well, what you're doing is very dangerous,' said the lifeguard. 'What are you doing wearing those?' pointing at Dangerous Dave's feet.

'Keeping my feet warm and dry' said Dangerous Dave. 'I don't like getting wet.'

'This is a swimming pool, sir' said the lifeguard with an irritated sound in his voice. 'You are going to get wet! But you can't wear socks in the swimming pool.'

'Why not?' said Dangerous Dave. 'There's not a rule on the signboard about it.'

'No, sir, there's not,' said the lifeguard. 'That's because everybody knows that you don't wear socks in the water. You could slip.'

'But I didn't slip, did I?' said Dangerous Dave.

'Out!' cried the lifeguard in a loud voice, and with this, Dangerous Dave scuttled off to the changing room, still wearing his socks.

'Where's dad?' said Sarah.

'I don't know,' said Will. 'Perhaps he's gone to get changed.'

And so off they went to the changing rooms. Will looked all around the changing room, but Dangerous Dave was not to be found.

'Have you seen my dad?' Will said to one of the cleaners in the changing room.

'What does he look like?' replied the cleaner.

'Well, he's about this high' said Will, with his hand stretched high for the cleaner to see. 'And he's got black hair, glasses, an old cream jumper and a fluffy hat.'

'Oh...' said the cleaner. 'I think he's in the coffee lounge.'

'The coffee lounge!' exclaimed Will.

'Yes,' said the cleaner. 'He didn't look very happy to me.'

Will quickly got himself changed, met Sarah outside the entrance and went to find Dangerous Dave. All their friends followed behind to see what had happened.

There, in the coffee lounge, was Dangerous Dave sat with a large black coffee (which was always his favourite), reading his book.

'Where have you been?' asked Sarah.

'I got thrown out the pool,' answered Dangerous Dave.

'How long have you been here?'

'Oh just a little while,' replied Dangerous Dave, but you could see from the smirk on his face that he was clearly lying.

'He's had two cups of coffee in the last ten minutes and shaking like a jelly' called the lady from behind the counter.

'Scared of the water, were we?' said Will.

'No,' said Dangerous Dave. 'I got told off for wearing my socks!'

'You wore your socks?!' exclaimed the children.

This was quickly followed by Sarah and her friends chanting 'scaredy cat, scaredy cat...' all the way home. Dangerous Dave was not very pleased.

Not many months later, Daphne had suggested to Dangerous Dave that they moved house. The last one was getting too big and Daphne was finding that it was too much work to keep it all clean and tidy. It had four gardens, a large lounge, two bathrooms – one with a Jacuzzi, a washroom, a big L-shaped kitchen, a downstairs bedroom and then three more gigantic bedrooms upstairs. It was a lot to clean!

So Daphne, Will and Sarah looked for a new house – somewhere in the countryside where they could look out on the fields and the forest, watch the ponies and see the train to London go along the tracks in the distance.

This house was much smaller and everyone seemed quite happy. Will and Sarah had smaller bedrooms too, but neither of them seemed to mind too much.

The new house still had two bathrooms; but there was a problem. There was no bath. Instead there was a shower.

It was a large, walk in, white shower with a special non-slip floor and a seat that you could sit on for when you were washing your hair. The shower head could be adjusted in height depending on whether you were big or little; and the large pane of glass at the side meant that you could use your finger and write messages in the condensation.

'It's easy to use,' the plumber had told Daphne. 'All you have to do is turn the two knobs. The first one is to turn it on and off. The second one is to change it from hot to cold.'

'That doesn't sound too difficult,' said Daphne.

'I don't think dad's going to like it,' said Will.

'Well, he'll have to like it,' said Sarah. 'He's got to keep himself clean.'

A few days passed and Dangerous Dave had been working very hard to avoid the shower as much as possible. You couldn't control a shower, you see, in the same way that you could control bath water.

He had taken a look at the two knobs and then decided that they looked a bit complicated so he might just avoid it and leave it for another day!

By the fifth day, Daphne, Will and Sarah had heard enough of the excuses. 'This evening you are going to have a shower,' said

Daphne. 'No more excuses. You need to get used to it.'

'I'll tell you how it works', said Will. 'You turn the first knob and that puts the water on and off. Then you turn the second knob and that changes the water from cold to hot. If you turn that knob halfway then the water will come out warm.'

'Go on, dad, you can do it,' said Sarah.

'I'm not happy,' said Dangerous Dave,' but if I must I must.' And with that he took himself off upstairs to get ready for his shower.

There was a lot of huffing and puffing going on as Dangerous

Dave went up the stairs, first in the bedroom and then finally into the bathroom. The light switch was turned on and the door firmly closed.

Downstairs in the living room, Daphne, Will and Sarah were all sat on the sofa, listening very quietly. The bathroom, you see, was above the living room, and if you were very quiet, you could hear the sound of the shower water landing on the shower base before going down the plughole and into the pipes that ran behind the living room fireplace.

'I think he's going to try it,' said Will.

'Let's see,' replied Sarah. 'He might just pretend to put the shower on and not actually go under it at all.'

They did not have to wait long. First there was the sound of the shower being turned on. Next came the sound of the water coming out the shower head and hitting the shower base... but the third sound was a little unexpected.

'Aaaaaaaaaaaaaaaaaaaaaaaaaaaaaah' came a sound from upstairs; and quickly the sound of fumbling could be heard as the water came to a sudden stop!

Daphne, Will and Sarah rushed to the bottom of the stairs and called up 'Are you okay?'

For a split second there was no answer. Then the door of the bathroom was open and out appeared a very wet looking Dangerous Dave.

'What was that scream about?' asked Will.

'I'm all wet,' replied Dangerous Dave.

'Yes,' said Will. 'That's what happens when you go for a shower.'

'But my pyjamas are all wet,' said Dangerous Dave.

'Your pyjamas?' said Sarah, looking most puzzled.

'And my slippers are all wet as well' said Dangerous Dave.

'Your slippers?' said Daphne with an equally puzzling look on her face.

'Please...' said Will taking a deep breath. 'Please tell me that you didn't go into the shower with your pyjamas and your slippers on.'

'Well of course I did,' said Dangerous Dave.

'WHY?' said Daphne.

'Well I only wanted to wash my hair!' said Dangerous Dave.

And my, what a wet sight he looked. His pyjamas were all dripping, his slippers were all wet and floppy; his hair looking like a bird had made a nest in it.

Daphne, Will and Sarah looked at each other very seriously; and seconds later laughed out loud as they couldn't contain it any longer.

'That's the last time I'm having a shower!' said Dangerous Dave.

But you'll be glad to know it wasn't – even if it did take some persuading to get him to try again!

Chapter 3

Dangerous Dave goes rowing

It was the Easter holidays and the children were off school for a couple of weeks. Daphne suggested that they went on a holiday to give everyone a break and to see somewhere different. Dangerous Dave liked the idea, but made it quite clear that he was not going abroad.

'People in other countries don't eat the right food,' he said. 'When they have bacon, eggs, sausages, tomatoes, mushrooms, beans, toast and black coffee, then I might think about going abroad.'

'Oh dad,' cried Will. 'People in many other countries do eat normal food. Take France, for example, they eat normal food. They make fresh bread, eat cheese, drink wine and have lots of the same food as we do.'

'No, they don't,' said Dangerous Dave. 'They eat frogs' legs!'

'Not all the time!' replied Sarah.

'I don't care,' said Dangerous Dave. 'If they eat frogs' legs, then I'm not going. Who knows what I would be eating if I went abroad! No, we shall stay in England.'

So, for the next few days, the family spent time trying to work out where they would like to go.

Daphne said she fancied going to Wales and seeing some of the beautiful castles, the little villages and the lovely coastline. Will said that he wanted to go up to London and see all the sights like Buckingham Palace, the Globe, the Science Museum and the street artists at Covent Garden. Sarah said that she fancied going to Cornwall to visit the Eden Project and sit on the cliff side at the Minack Theatre.

Dangerous Dave however had his mind set on other things. 'Let's go to the Lake District,' he said. 'We could hire a little holiday home in Keswick and then we could explore the mountains and go out on the lakes. It would be a lot of fun.'

'It's a long way to drive,' said Daphne.

'That's alright,' said Dangerous Dave. 'You can manage it!' and with that he walked off with a contended grin on his face.

Within hours, the Keswick Tourist Information Centre had been contacted and the all-important brochure was on its way in the post.

Dangerous Dave was so excited when the brochure arrived.

'Look,' he said. 'There's a lovely little cottage in Keswick. It's called Daffodil Cottage and look at all the lovely flowers outside. It's got a kitchen, a bathroom, a living room, and two bedrooms and a....'

'Two bedrooms!' cried Sarah. 'That's not enough'.

'Yes it is,' said Dangerous Dave. 'You and Will can share a room. It won't hurt for just a week.'

'Only if we can have pillow fights and sock fights', said Will.

'Yeah,' said Sarah, changing her mind. 'We could have midnight feasts as well!'

'Well, go and phone them,' said Daphne, 'and see if the cottage is available – although I must admit it does look a bit small.'

Dangerous Dave went off and dialled the number on the telephone. He spoke very loudly to the lady down the other end of the line. This was not unusual as Dangerous Dave seemed to have the idea that if you couldn't see the person you were talking to, then you had to shout so that the other person could hear. As much as Daphne, Will and Sarah tried to explain that the telephone worked without having to shout down it, Dangerous Dave was still not convinced.

He came off the phone from the lady at Daffodil Cottage with a big smile on his face. 'The cottage is free and we can arrive on Friday.'

When Friday came, there was a mixture of emotions in the house. Daphne was busy still packing clothes in the suitcases for Will, Sarah, Dangerous Dave and herself. Will was putting his writing pad, his toys, his music player and his sweets into the backseat of the car. Sarah was walking around her bedroom with her headphones on listening to music. Dangerous Dave was sat at the table, drinking black coffee and studying the map.

'It shouldn't take long,' he exclaimed. 'About five hours I reckon. Just a tuppeny ha'penny bus ride.'

Eventually, everyone was ready. Daphne sat in the driving seat and after six long hours they eventually reached Keswick.

Daffodil Cottage was small. It was a terrace cottage trapped in between Tulip Cottage and Carnation Cottage. The walls were painted yellow and the wallpaper inside the house was a pale yellow colour too.

'I see why they called it Daffodil Cottage,' said Sarah. 'Everything is yellow!'

Inside the kitchen however there was a basket of fruit and vegetables, a box of chocolates and a bottle of wine waiting for them.

'That's nice,' said Dangerous Dave. 'Just what I needed!' and with that he sat down on the sofa with the chocolates and a glass of wine; leaving Daphne, Will and Sarah to bring in all the luggage from the car.

The next morning the sun was shining and everyone was feeling much happier. They had all slept well and were keen to get some exercise going after sitting in the car for most of the previous day.

'Let's go mountain climbing,' said Dangerous Dave.

'No, not today,' replied Daphne. 'Let's not injure ourselves on the first main day of the holiday.'

'Okay, said Dangerous Dave, 'let's go down to the lake then.'

So off they set. They walked through the town of Keswick, past the old museum and the little supermarket, and down to the lakeside.

The lake was extremely long and stretched for miles. Standing on the edge of the lake you could see the other side, but if you looked to the left the lake kept going and going and going. You couldn't see the end in sight.

'Let's have a coffee,' suggested Dangerous Dave, which was always the first thing to do whenever you went anywhere.

'We only had breakfast half an hour ago,' said Daphne.

'I know,' replied Dangerous Dave. 'But I fancy a coffee.'

So off they went into the little coffee house on the side of the lake. Dangerous Dave had an extra-large black coffee and a toasted teacake. Daphne had a cup of tea and the children had hot chocolates!

'I think it's time we went for a row,' said Dangerous Dave.

'Do you know how to row?' said Sarah.

'Of course I do' answered Dangerous Dave. 'When your brother was young, I used to be a scout master and we would bring all the scouts up here every year. We did lots of exciting things at camp including climbing mountains and rowing and much more. You have no need to be worried with me around.'

'Are you coming rowing, mum?' said Will, hopeful that if Dangerous Dave did have any problems that Daphne would be able to save the situation.

'No, I'm going to stay here,' replied Daphne. 'I have got a bit of a headache after all that driving yesterday. I could take some photos of you in the rowing boat though.'

'Come on then,' said Sarah excitedly. 'Let's go rowing.'

Dangerous Dave, Will and Sarah headed down to the edge of the lake to find the man hiring out the rowing boats, leaving Daphne behind in the tearoom.

The owner of the rowing boats was a very big man with rippling muscles. He wore a pair of corduroy trousers and an old white t-shirt. His big toes were short and stubby as they protruded from the brown flip-flops that were sliding on and off his feet.

'How long do you want?' he asked.

'Ummm...about an hour I suppose,' replied Dangerous Dave, handing him the money.

'Hop in,' he said, 'and I'll give you a shove.'

Dangerous Dave, Will and Sarah got into the boat. Dangerous Dave gripped the oars and prepared himself for the great rowing adventure.

The man gave the rowing boat a big shove out into the lake. Dangerous Dave did a big heave on the oars and immediately brought the little boat back into land.

The man looked a little surprised. 'Sorry,' said Dangerous Dave.

'Not a problem, mate' said the man. 'I'll give you another big shove in just a second.'

So Dangerous Dave practised his movements with the oars to ensure that this time he got it right.

The man returned and gave the little boat another big shove. Dangerous Dave gripped the oars, swung widely and immediately the little boat started moving through the water… back towards the shore again.

This time the man did not look pleased! His freckled face had started to turn red, his eyebrows raised with a disapproving stare and a walk towards the little boat that spoke of there being consequences if this happened again.

Dangerous Dave let out a little apologetic smile and took the oars again. For the third time the man gave the little boat another shove into the lake. Dangerous Dave fumbled with the oars and managed to get the little boat to go a little further out from the shore.

'At last,' shouted Sarah. 'Now we can go for a proper row.'

'Got to turn the boat to the right first,' said Dangerous Dave, his voice now sounding like that of an expert and as if nothing had previously happened at all.

With a few swings on just one of the oars the little boat had turned left and was facing the small village of Keswick not far off in the distance.

'We will go up this end first,' said Dangerous Dave to Will and Sarah. 'We don't want to go too far the other end and not have enough time to get back in time.'

'Okay Dad,' said Will.

The little boat started moving through the water with Dangerous Dave doing his best to manage the oars. As far as Will and Sarah could see, Dangerous Dave clearly hadn't done much rowing ever in his life. As for the scouts that he had in years past brought to Keswick, well, who knows what happened to them!

'We're getting rather close to that person's back garden,' said Sarah, noticing that the boat was getting very close to the shore, just a short distance away from the place where they had upset the rowing boat owner.

'It's fine. I know what I'm doing. I will turn the boat round in a minute,' answered Dangerous Dave.

'You could just row the oars in the opposite direction,' suggested Will.

'No!' replied Dangerous Dave. 'How would I see where we are going? No, whenever you are rowing, you have to turn the boat round so that you can see what's ahead.'

'Okay, dad,' said Will, not totally convinced that Dangerous Dave knew what he was talking about. After all, why couldn't you look over your shoulder to see what's behind you?

As the boat started to turn, there was a crunching sound from underneath the boat and it came to an immediate stop.

'What's happened?' asked Sarah.

'We've run aground' said Will.

'We're okay,' said Dangerous Dave. 'I'll get us out of this in a jiffy.'

He pushed on the left oar but the little boat wouldn't move.

He pushed on the right oar but the little boat refused to budge.

He pushed on both oars but still the little boat maintained its position. They were stuck.

'I could stick my leg out of the boat and push against the edge of the ground' suggested Will.

'Oh no, you don't,' replied Dangerous Dave. 'We don't want to do anything dangerous, do we? What would your mum say?'

And so for the next few minutes they sat there wondering what to do.

In the meantime, Daphne had come out of the tearoom, ready to take some photos with her camera of Dangerous Dave, Will and Sarah in the rowing boat.

'Where are they?' she said to herself, looking out across the lake. 'I can't see them anywhere.'

She walked down to the little boatshed, but they weren't there. She walked along the edge of the lake for a short distance but there was still no sign of them. Finally she walked up the slope that passed by the neighbouring house and as she looked, she saw a little rowing boat with a man and two children stranded in the corner of the lake, right by the neighbour's back garden.

Daphne laughed and laughed. She had never laughed so much in all her life. To the left of her was miles and miles of endless lake and here was her husband no further away than the neighbour's back garden, stranded in his boat that had run aground! Only Dangerous Dave, she thought to herself, could have got the little rowing boat stuck there.

Back at the boathouse, the owner was wondering where boat 22 had disappeared to. He looked at his list. Boat 22 should have been back about twenty five minutes ago. He looked down at the list in his cabin, scratching his head, trying to think of who had hired boat number 22. Then he remembered. It was that man with the two children who had kept rowing himself in rather than out.

'Oh no,' he thought to himself. 'What's he done?'

With no time to lose, the boat owner jumped into another one of his rowing boats and started to row out onto the lake to see if he could see boat number 22. He didn't have to go far before he spotted Dangerous Dave.

'Great,' he said to himself sarcastically. 'The next door

neighbour is definitely not going to be pleased.'

He rowed his boat close, but not too close, to boat number 22. He got out of his boat and waded in the water to get to Dangerous Dave, Will and Sarah.

'Hello,' said Dangerous Dave.

The man didn't reply. He gave the children a smile, but stared intensely at Dangerous Dave.

'Right,' he said. 'I am going to give you a big shove so that you can get out of here.'

He stood behind the boat and gave it a big shove, not just once, twice, but three times. Each time there was a little creaking noise, but the boat refused to move. The man tried again and again; his face turning redder and redder.

'It's like that story of the Enormous Turnip' said Sarah. 'They all heaved and heaved.'

'Be quiet,' said Dangerous Dave.

'Sorry...' said Sarah, although both she and Will found the idea rather funny. Dangerous Dave just sat there starring out across the lake.

'Right,' said the man. 'I am going to get a rope from my boat and tie it to your boat. Then when I count 1, 2, 3, I shall row my boat and you push on the oars on your boat.'

'Right!' replied Dangerous Dave.

So the man attached the rope between the two boats before getting in his own boat.

'1, 2, 3...' shouted the man. 'Push'.

Dangerous Dave pushed on the oars, but not in the right direction. The rope came undone and the man's face turned even redder.

'Give me the oars!' he said to Dangerous Dave. 'Now this time I shall just pull you to shore from my boat,' he said. 'I don't think I trust you with the oars anymore, sir.'

Dangerous Dave looked slightly hurt.

The man tied the rope again and got back into his own boat. He pulled on the oars and slowly boat number 22 gradually came away from the ground and back onto the water.

The man heaved and puffed as he rowed his own boat with the weight of boat number 22 (and Dangerous Dave and Will and Sarah) behind him until they got back to the boathouse.

'Thank you very much,' said Dangerous Dave as they got out of the little boat. 'It was most enjoyable.'

The man grunted and didn't say anything.

Daphne had come down to meet them.

'I wondered where you had gone,' she said.

'You'll never guess,' said Will.

'Oh, I will,' she said. 'I saw you trapped in the corner there. I also saw the man come and rescue you. Look, here's the photos on my camera.'

Will and Sarah looked at the photos and everybody laughed apart from Dangerous Dave.

'Can we go rowing again tomorrow?' asked Sarah. 'I would like to go down the lake.'

'Okay,' said Will, 'but this time I will do the rowing.'

'Hmmmph' said Dangerous Dave.
'It's a black coffee for me!'

Chapter 4

Dangerous Dave and the Ants

Dangerous Dave was never too interested in doing jobs around the house. If he mended anything then someone else would normally have to come and repair the same thing that Dangerous Dave had tried to do himself.

When it came to washing and ironing the clothes, it was Daphne's job. When it came to changing Veka the cat's litter, it was Daphne's job. When it was time to do the gardening, that also was Daphne's job – although standing outside with the garden hose was sometimes acceptable to Dangerous Dave. It gave him a good opportunity to be out of the house, doing something useful, and giving him the opportunity to think and dream about becoming a millionaire one day!

Jobs like dusting, putting 'Henry' hoover around, cleaning the windows or doing other such work was also not of Dangerous Dave's concern. He was the man of the house and therefore, in his opinion, these jobs did not need to be done by him.

One particular morning Dangerous Dave got up out of bed, ready to go and work in his little tool shop, and headed off for the kitchen for his first coffee of the morning.

He picked up his favourite glass mug, opened the cutlery drawer and took out a teaspoon. Then he reached for the coffee jar that always sat right next to the kettle, just in case an emergency coffee was needed, and put a large teaspoon of Columbian coffee granules into the bottom of the mug. The kettle was then filled with water and put on ready to boil. Both Dangerous Dave and the kettle whistled happily together as both waited for each other for the next move.

The hot water was poured into the glass mug and the smile on

Dangerous Dave's face grew wider and wider as he smelt the coffee aroma and prepared for his first sip. There was only one thing missing – sugar.

Dangerous Dave looked around for the sugar bowl. It wasn't in its normal place next to the glass mugs.

'Hmmmm,' he thought to himself. 'Now where's that gone?'

He looked behind the glass mugs but it wasn't there. He searched behind the toaster but it wasn't there either. He investigated along the spice shelf, but it wasn't there either. That meant there was only one place it could have been put – in the larder.

With no time to lose, Dangerous Dave swung open the larder door. There, right at the front, on the bottom shelf, sat the sugar pot. He was just about to pick it up when he noticed that some of the sugar granules had gone black.

'That's strange,' he thought to himself. 'What's happened here?'

As he picked up the sugar pot to take a closer look, he saw that the black things were moving around.

'Oh no,' he cried. 'It's ants. There's ants in the sugar.'

He put the teaspoon into the sugar pot and tried to lift one or two of them out, but this was not very easy as the ants kept playing 'hide and seek' within the sugar.

'What am I going to do without my coffee?' cried Dangerous Dave.

He sat there for nearly thirty seconds thinking hard about what to do next. 'Well,' he thought to himself. 'I can't do without my coffee – and my coffee can't do without sugar.' And with that, Dangerous Dave picked up the teaspoon again, put it into the sugar bowl, lifted out a couple of teaspoons of sugar (and ants) and dropped them into his coffee.

'It won't hurt,' said Dangerous Dave. 'A couple of dead ants in the bottom of the mug is fine and I can still enjoy my coffee!'

The first sip was delicious and there was no evidence of any dead ants having gone through the coffee or the sugar at all. In fact the taste was just a little better than normal. Perhaps ants added some kind of gritty taste to the coffee; the kind of taste that Dangerous Dave particularly liked.

Quite satisfied, Dangerous Dave picked up the sugar pot and went to put it back into the larder where he had found it. But as he put it back in, he noticed that there were a lot of little black things running all about the larder, going in and out of all the food.

There were hundreds of ants who were all having an amazing time. They were climbing up and down the dry spaghetti, scrambling their way through the cornflakes in the box, playing motor racing round the jars and tins and even playing 'peekaboo' between the 'Rich Tea' biscuits.

'Oh no,' thought Dangerous Dave. 'What am I going to do? I've got to go to work in a minute and I mustn't disturb Daphne as she's still asleep.'

His mind thought hard. Now most people at this point would have had the sensible idea of taking the food out of the larder; throwing away any of the food which had ants in it; putting some ant powder around the larder; and killing any of the ants that had escaped by clinging onto the packets, jars and tins. But not Dangerous Dave, no,...another plan came to his mind!

'What I need to do,' thought Dangerous Dave, 'is to stop them enjoying themselves any further. If they leave the larder then goodness knows what they will do next.'

And with that, Dangerous Dave opened the bottom drawer in the kitchen and started rummaging through all the items to find the one thing he knew he needed.

The bottom drawer was one of those places that kept all sorts of bits and bobs – the things that you don't really know where to put, so they end up in the bottom drawer until the day where someone says 'Oh I need a piece of string' and then someone else says 'It's in the bottom drawer I think.'

There were spare plugs, fuses, old elastic bands, instruction manuals for various devices in the house, screwdrivers of all different shapes and sizes, pieces of Blu-Tack, a pair of garden scissors, a ball of green wool and various nails, screws and bolts.

Dangerous Dave shuffled all these things around in the drawer whilst he continued to search for the very item he was looking for – and eventually he found it. Brown parcel tape!

Very quickly, the tape was lifted out, the drawer closed and the kitchen scissors ready for action. Dangerous Dave cut an enormously long piece of brown parcel tape and then another and then another. Then taking as much care as possible, he took the first piece and stuck it to the side of the larder door. The second piece he stuck to the top of the door and the third piece to the bottom of the door. Dangerous Dave then tried opening the larder door. It moved a little bit, but you certainly couldn't open it any further.

'Hmmm,' thought Dangerous Dave, 'not quite good enough.'

And with that the scissors started work again as three more long pieces of brown parcel tape were cut and positioned over the top of the last three pieces of parcel tape. Then, with curiosity, Dangerous Dave tried opening the larder door again. This time it didn't even try to move. The door was now well and truly fixed closed.

'That solves the problem,' said Dangerous Dave. 'Now those ants won't be going anywhere!'

And with that, Dangerous Dave put away the brown parcel tape and the scissors, drank the last part of his coffee and set off out the back door to go to his little tool shop.

It was about half an hour later when Daphne walked into the kitchen. It was school holidays and Will and Sarah were busily playing in their rooms. To start with, Daphne did not notice the brown tape on the larder door. She went to the airing cupboard, pulled out a tablecloth with white, orange and yellow squares on it and put it onto the table. Then she went to the top drawer of the kitchen and took out some knives and teaspoons and laid them out in their designated places. Then she took out some glass tumblers, fetched the blackcurrant squash from the drinks cupboard; filled the glasses with the squash and some cold water from the tap before putting these onto the table as well.

'What would you like for breakfast?' she cried to Will.

'Milupa, mum, please,' replied Will.

Milupa was intended to be a breakfast cereal for babies, but

Will had been eating it for breakfast for many years and still hadn't grown out of the white, spongy-like cereal that came in all different flavours.

'And what do you want, Sarah?' asked Daphne.

'Coco Pops please,' replied Sarah.

It was at that moment that Daphne set off towards the larder. She pulled at the door, having still not noticed the brown parcel tape. The door wouldn't open. Daphne was surprised and then, as she looked at the side, top and bottom of the door, she spotted the brown parcel tape.

'What's this doing here?' she asked herself. She called to Will and Sarah.

'Do you know why there's brown parcel tape round the larder door?'

'No,' replied Will, who came to have a look.

'What's dad done this time?' replied Sarah, who likewise also came to have a look. 'It does seem very strange,' she added.

Carefully, Daphne took the kitchen scissors and started to cut away at the brown parcel tape. It was quite difficult to cut through two layers of sticky tape, but eventually the tape was off and Daphne started to open the door.

Inside was now thousands, not hundreds, of little black ants running all over the place.

'Ants,' cried Daphne.

'Thousands of them,' exclaimed Will.

'But why did Dangerous Dave tape the door?' questioned Sarah.

For the next hour, Daphne, Will and Sarah worked hard, removing all the food and killing off all the ants. The perishable food was thrown into the outdoor bin, whilst the non-perishable food was packed into cardboard boxes and placed into the washroom.

Ant powder was positioned all over the larder and slowly, but surely, the ants were killed and removed from the larder.

When Dangerous Dave came home from work, the expression on his face was smiling; but it changed very quickly when Daphne held up a piece of old, brown parcel tape.

'What's this all about?' she asked quite adamantly.

'Oh that....' replied Dangerous Dave. 'That was because there were ants in the larder.'

'I know that!' answered Daphne, 'but what was the tape doing to solve the problem?'

'Keeping the ants in so they didn't escape,' said Dangerous Dave with a look of genius on his face.

'Keeping the ants in!' cried Daphne. 'They were crawling in and out of all our food; and you just let them stay there and have a picnic!'

'Well I didn't want them to bother you,' said Dangerous Dave.

'Listen,' said Daphne. 'The next time you see ants, you have to remove all the food and kill the ants; not just trap them in the larder. Do you understand?'

'Yes,' said Dangerous Dave apologetically. 'I'm sorry.' He paused. 'But do you think we could just keep one or two of them?'

'What for?' said Will and Sarah together.

'Well,...' said Dangerous Dave slowly, 'they do taste quite nice in black coffee!'

There was silence for about five seconds before everybody started to laugh.

'Okay,' said Daphne. 'But just one or two, no more.'

'Great!' said Dangerous Dave, and with that he put the kettle on again.

Chapter 5

Dangerous Dave and Nutty Nanny

Nutty Nanny was Dangerous Dave's mum. She was one of the nicest ladies you could ever know. She lived in a little flat in Trinidad Mansions with lots of other elderly people who used to enjoy going out for little strolls, looking at the squirrels racing up and down the trees, or going to buy some fish tit-bits for the local cats whom they would stroke and have a little chat with. Every cat was important and could not be ignored.

People who lived at Trinidad Mansions weren't allowed pets of their own so they enjoyed seeing all the animals that came wandering into the back garden from the houses behind.

From Nutty Nanny's kitchen window you could see into the back house's garden where there was a large outdoor swimming pool, and you could see the children splashing and having fun. It reminded Nutty Nanny of when she was young.

Nutty Nanny had been given her nickname by Will and Sarah because of some of the strange things she also did; although they weren't quite as unusual as Dangerous Dave.

Every Friday afternoon, after school, it was either Will or Sarah's turn to go to tea with Nutty Nanny. This usually followed the same routine. The first thing to do was to build a den with all the old brown chairs, the big pieces of cardboard that she hid in the cupboard, the bed sheets and some of the cushions or pillows. If permission was given, clothes belts, sellotape and string were also added into making the den to provide extra security and defence.

Once the den had been built, Nutty Nanny would start to go

and prepare the tea whilst Will or Sarah would sit inside the den reading 'Beano' comics or gaze through some of the old magazines that lived in the cupboard on the right hand side of the living room cabinet.

The tea would then be ready. Usually it was served on the 'birdie' plate where there was a picture of a blue tit on the bottom of the plate covered over by the food. Only by eating all of your dinner would you get to see the bird at the bottom. It was a sneaky ploy to make sure that Will and Sarah actually ate all their dinner, but it did seem to work.

The dinner was usually something quite simple that was accompanied by mashed potato and tinned spaghetti shapes. Usually it was either minced beef, 'Campbell's Meatballs' or 'Birds Eye Fish Fingers'.

The thing was, however, that Nutty Nanny was not the world's greatest cook. If she cooked minced beef, then it was usually grey by the time that it was served and all the goodness had been drained out of it. If it was 'Campbell's Meatballs' then they would have been boiled to death and came out with large bubbles in the sauce that accompanied them. Or if it was 'Birds Eye Fish Fingers' then most of the fish would be outside of the breadcrumbs, having escaped out of the finger shape in a pure attempt to avoid being cooked any further. Will and Sarah however didn't really seem to mind.

Immediately after dinner, it was time to watch the television. This would be three half hour programmes in succession. The first would be 'Thunderbirds' followed by 'Top Gear' and finally the quiz show 'Family Fortunes'. Quite why Nutty Nanny liked 'Top Gear', considering she had never learned to drive nor ever needed to, was a bit of a mystery.

Both Will and Sarah would sit incredibly close to the screen. Whilst this is bad for your eyes, it was very important at Nutty Nanny's as the volume was kept at an all-time low so sitting close to the screen was the only way to ever hear anything that was being said. Nutty Nanny however would sit on the sofa and make up the storyline in her own mind. She would even do this with murder mysteries!

Nutty Nanny was good fun to be with, even though her flat did look like a bomb had probably hit the place by the time Daphne came to collect them.

One day Nutty Nanny arrived at Will and Sarah's house. Daphne opened the door and invited her in for some tea. It was not unusual for Nutty Nanny to visit as she enjoyed the company and was particularly keen on Dangerous Dave's family.

'I was wondering if you would all like to come to Sunday tea,' she said, hopeful that they would all say 'yes'. 'I've made a lovely chocolate sponge with butter icing in the middle.'

'Oh please can we go?' said Sarah, who knew that if there was one thing Nutty Nanny could cook, it was chocolate sponge.

'Sunday should be fine,' replied Daphne.

'Good,' said Nutty Nanny. 'I've also found this new recipe which I am going to try and I'll be interested to know your opinions.'

'Oh dear,' said Dangerous Dave.

'Okay,' said Will, wondering quite what this new recipe could be.

And with that, Nutty Nanny put on her pink woollen hat that she always wore, said her farewells and made her way back to Trinidad Mansions.

Three days went by and Sunday finally arrived. In the morning, Dangerous Dave took the family off to the church where they went every Sunday. From there they would go down to the local park for a coffee (of course!) and to feed the ducks with the leftover bread. Then it was home where a roast dinner would be prepared before sitting down and watching some afternoon television or playing a family board game. At 4:30pm it was time to go to Trinidad Mansions to have tea with Nutty Nanny.

When they arrived, the flat was tidier than normal. The feather duster had been put round and the old carpet sweeper had clearly made some attempt at picking up (or dropping) some of the bits on the floor. Nutty

Nanny stood at the door, smiling, and welcoming them inside.

On the living room table, surrounded by five brown chairs, was all sorts of food that Nutty Nanny had prepared. There was bread and butter, some homemade jam tarts, the chocolate sponge with the butter icing in the middle, some pieces of cheese and some 'Wotsit' crisps in a bowl. Everyone sat down at the table, looking both content and eager with the food prepared before them.

'Very good, mum,' said Dangerous Dave. 'But where's the new recipe you mentioned?'

'Oh… good thing you mentioned it, I nearly forgot them,' she said. And with that, she wandered off into her little kitchen.

She returned carrying a plate with what can only be described as some dark brown lumps sat on them. They were twisted and curled and looked as solid as a rock. 'I made these especially for you,' Nutty Nanny exclaimed with great joy.

'Errr.. what are they?' asked Will.

'They're a new recipe,' said Nutty Nanny. 'They're called Chocolate Rockies'.

'Chocolate rockies?!' cried Dangerous Dave. 'They look like rocks too. Here, let's cover them up with this napkin.' And that's what he did.

'Now don't be unkind,' said Daphne. 'I am sure they are quite fine', although you could tell from the look on her face that Daphne was definitely not going to try one.

The tea on the whole was quite good, until Dangerous Dave decided that he would be brave and try one of the chocolate rockies. He took one bite into it, but the rocky didn't want to be bit into. He tried again, but still the rocky did not want to be consumed. He took one last enormous bite and snap, the front of his tooth broke off.

'Oh no,' said Dangerous Dave. 'I've broken a tooth.'

'Oh I am sorry,' said Nutty Nanny, quite apologetically. 'I did wonder if they were going to be okay. You see, when I was making them on Friday evening, there was a powercut and all the lights went off and I couldn't really see what I was doing; so I just had to hope for the best. I must admit...' she added, 'they didn't really want to come off the baking tin.'

'I see,' said Dangerous Dave.

A few months later it was coming up to Lent. Nutty Nanny, who had got over the bad experience of the chocolate rockies, had had another idea.

'It's Shrove Tuesday next week,' she said. 'I think I will make some pancakes.'

So off she went round to the local shop to buy some pancake mix. As she went, she went through the little gate that out of the back of Trinidad Mansions; past the bus-stop where the Rossmore Flyer would stop; past the shoe shop and the drinks shop, across the main road and into the little Spar shop on the other side.

Nutty Nanny had never used pancake mix before, but she was pretty convinced that she could make pancakes if she took her time and really thought about it.

She paid the 89p for the mixture and started to make her way back home, stopping off only at the fish and chip shop down in the alley to buy some more fish tit-bits for the cats whom she would go to find later that afternoon.

On arriving home, she sat down to look at the recipe. It didn't seem too hard. The packet said that you just had to mix a few ingredients together whilst cooking it on the little Babybel hob she had in her kitchen.

Nutty Nanny's kitchen was not very big. In fact you probably couldn't swing a cat in there. It had enough room for the tiny hob, a little sink, a small table with two chairs and a few cupboards tucked away in the corner. The fridge was a portable one that sat in the corner of the worktop. Nutty Nanny was quite pleased therefore that there wasn't too much preparation to do in making pancakes.

All was going well until it was time to flip the pancakes. According to the recipe, you simply held the frying pan, flipped the pancake into the air, caught it again in the pan and continued to cook.

'Well, here goes,' said Nutty Nanny – and with that, she flipped the pancake up into the air. She held out the frying pan to catch it, but no pancake arrived back in the pan.

'Hmmm,' thought Nutty Nanny, rather puzzled. 'Now where did that go?'

She looked up at the ceiling but the pancake wasn't there. The doorbell rang, so Nutty Nanny walked with the frying pan in her hand to answer it. It was Dangerous Dave.

'Oh come in,' said Nutty Nanny. 'I've lost my pancake.'

'How have you lost a pancake?' said Dangerous Dave.

'I don't know,' said Nutty Nanny. 'I flipped it and then it disappeared.'

So, Nutty Nanny and Dangerous Dave started to look around the kitchen to find it. They looked on the floor, but it wasn't there. They searched around the cupboards, under the table, on the table, behind the fridge, on the windowsill, and all over the place, but still the pancake was missing.

'Bend over' said Dangerous Dave to Nutty Nanny.

'Why?' answered Nutty Nanny.

'In case it's on your head,' replied Dangerous Dave, but it wasn't on Nutty Nanny's head either.

'Perhaps I never made one,' doubted Nutty Nanny. 'Perhaps I

thought I had made one and I hadn't.'

'But the mixture packet is all empty,' said Dangerous Dave, 'you must have done something with it.'

'Well I don't know what I've done,' said Nutty Nanny. 'Never mind... I shall just have to clear up later.'

For about the next twenty minutes Nutty Nanny and Dangerous Dave sat down for a drink and a chat whilst still trying to work out the mystery of the missing pancake in their minds. After that, Dangerous Dave left to go home and Nutty Nanny went into the kitchen to wash up the frying pan and other utensils.

The soapy water in the sink was already getting cold so Nutty Nanny added some hot water from the kettle into the water. She picked up the frying pan and lowered it into the sink. As she did, she felt something slippery at the bottom of the sink. She picked up the slithery thing and pulled it out of the water.

'Oh,' she said surprised. 'It's my pancake. That's where it went. When I flipped it, it must have flown through the air, splashed into the water and landed in the bottom of the sink.'

There was a moment of joy as she realised that she was quite so nutty after all.

'Perhaps I could have that for my tea...'

Chapter 6

Dangerous Dave and the Decking

Out the back of the little house in Larchington Close where Dangerous Dave and his family lived was a small garden. It had an L-shaped decking area, a small ornamental stone and rock area, a border garden and a small area of lawn. All around the garden were lots of sculptures of all sorts of things including running men, spiders, stained glass windows, bluebells, pheasants and birds. Daphne and Sarah were both very keen on sculpture and it made the garden more interesting.

Dangerous Dave's favourite part of the garden was the decking. Every year Dangerous Dave would say:

'I'm going to paint the decking this summer.'

And every year, Daphne, Will and Sarah would say:

'Okay, if you want to.'

And so Dangerous Dave would take himself outside and lay an old sheet on the decking boards. Then, with his old cream cardigan on (affectionately known to Dangerous Dave as 'wumpy') he would start to get the sandpaper and start rubbing down the individual boards. There were a lot of boards to do, but

Dangerous Dave didn't mind. It gave him a reason to be outside, minding his own business, and getting a useful job achieved.

The rubbing down of the boards, in between wet weather, coffee breaks, going to work, going to play darts, visiting the local town and all the other things Dangerous Dave would do, would take quite a few weeks. But eventually the day would arrive when it was time to get the paint out and start painting.

Next door lived Dougie, his wife Truly and the dog Snuffles. They were fairly quiet people but could sometimes be quite nosey as to what was going on. Snuffles, in particular, became disturbed by everything. If a plane flew over, he barked. If a train went along the train line at the far end of the field, behind the houses in the close, he would bark. If another dog barked, he would bark – and so slowly everything got used to the sound of a barking dog most of the day.

On this particular day, Dangerous Dave was out painting the decking boards. The reddish brown paint was splattering this way and that way by quite a small brush (meaning the job would conveniently take longer) as Dangerous Dave happily sat on his painting sheet, moving the paint up and down.

Dougie popped his head over the fence. 'You all right, Dave?' he asked.

'Yes, fine,' replied Dangerous Dave. 'Just doing the decking.'

'You ought to watch yourself,' said Dougie. 'It's going to take you ages like that. I'd get rid of all that decking if it was me. Cut it all down – good for the bonfire,' he continued.

'No, I like my decking,' said Dangerous Dave and he carried on painting.

When the job was all finished, Dangerous Dave would look at it with a great sense of pride. In the house he would walk with his hair all dotted with brown paint, along with patches over his 'wumpy', his green shorts, his bare knees and his socks and shoes.

'Looks like you painted yourself as well,' said Sarah.

'Don't be cheeky,' replied Dangerous Dave. 'Now what do you think?'

Daphne, Will and Sarah all gathered together at the patio windows to have a look.

'It's an improvement,' said Daphne.

'Yes, not bad,' said Will. 'I think you missed a bit though.'

'Where?' said Dangerous Dave indignantly.

'Only joking!' said Will.

And so the decking looked quite nice for the remainder of the summer. The problem was that by the time it got to the winter, the decking didn't look very different from how it had been before Dangerous Dave had painted it. The cold weather, the damp, the frost and the birds had got to it and white patches and bare pieces of wood were beginning to show through again.

Early into the next year Dangerous Dave had been unwell and spent some time in the hospital. He therefore needed quite a few weeks to recover.

'I'm looking forward to doing the decking though,' said Dangerous Dave.

'Oh no you don't,' said Daphne. 'You need to look after yourself. You can't be doing the decking this year.'

'But it needs doing!' said Dangerous Dave.

'It's alright,' said Will. 'I can do it this year. I've watched you enough times and I can probably get it just as good.'

'I'll show you the paint,' said Dangerous Dave as he and Will went out into the garage. He took a big tub from the back corner shelf and handed it to Will.

'That's the paint you need,' he said.

Will took one look inside the paint and frowned. The brown paint looked like muddy water. It was very sloppy and splashed against the side of the tub.

'No wonder this paint washes off so easily,' thought Will. 'I need to find some paint that will really stick onto the decking for ages.'

So whilst Dangerous Dave was out, Will decided to explore all the tubs of paint at the back of the garage. Most of them were for painting bedroom walls and other indoor jobs, until eventually Will found a tub of pinky-brown paint. He opened the tub to have a look. This paint was thick. It was sticky and it was absolutely perfect for the job.

'Excellent,' said Will to himself. 'I shall paint the decking with that!'

So for the next week, Will painted the pinky-brown paint all over the decking. The job was completed quite quickly and even Dangerous Dave had to admit that it looked quite good; although he wasn't totally convinced about the slightly pinky look.

'What paint did you use?' asked Dangerous Dave.

'This one,' said Will proudly, holding up the tub.

'That's stone paint!' said Dangerous Dave. 'You shouldn't be using this paint on wood.'

'Well it stays on the stone,' said Will. 'So why shouldn't it stay on the decking?'

'We'll see,' said Dangerous Dave sceptically.

Well, the winter came and the paint still stayed on the decking. The spring came and still the paint looked nice on the decking.

Dougie poked his nose over the garden fence. 'You all right, Dave?' he asked.

'Yes, feeling much better now thank you.'

'The decking is looking good,' said Dougie. 'Although I don't think the pinky colour is quite right for decking.'

'Will did it,' said Dangerous Dave.

'Well that explains it,' said Dougie, and with that his head disappeared back over into number 5.

The problem then came in the summer. The heat of the sun started to cause the paint to peel off the decking boards and now it really did look untidy.

'I'm going to do the decking,' said Dangerous Dave, 'and this year I'm doing it. No more pink muck on my decking boards!'

Out came the sheet, the sand paper, 'wumpy' and the tin of thin, brown paper. Dangerous Dave rubbed and scrubbed with the sand paper to get the pink paint off, but it didn't want to come. It was truly stuck on the decking.

'Blow it,' said Dangerous Dave. 'I'm going to have to get an industrial sander.' And within minutes he was on the telephone to the local hire company in Wareford to organise the loan of a sander.

Dangerous Dave had never used an industrial sander but it sounded easy enough. It was a big machine (nearly up to waist height on Dangerous Dave) on wheels with a conveyor belt on the bottom which moved the sanding paper to then sand off the paint from the decking. It simply needed plugging in, turning on and steering around the decking using the handlebars at the back. No different really from manoeuvring a shopping trolley around the supermarket – just a little bit heavier and a little bit noisier.

The men from the hire company arrived on the Tuesday morning and brought the industrial sander down the drive, through the little side gate and onto the decking. Dangerous Dave gave the machine a quick look over and decided that this was going to be easy and take no time at all.

The men asked if he needed any help, but Dangerous Dave told them that he was more than capable of using the machine and that they could collect it later that afternoon. With that, the men left and promised to come back later.

Dangerous Dave took the plug and plugged it in behind the palm plant in the living room just next to the patio door. He then went outside, put the cable safely around his shoulders and pressed the 'start' button.

The machine made a loud whirring noise and started to vibrate. The conveyor belt got busy sanding the wood underneath it; but when Dangerous Dave tried to move it, the machine wouldn't move. It just carried on sanding the same spot before there was a strange clunking noise and then everything went quiet.

'I wonder what has happened,' said Dangerous Dave.

He tried to turn the machine on again, but nothing was working. He tipped the machine on its side and then saw a problem.

'It's sanded a big dent in the decking,' said Dangerous Dave, 'and it's even sanded the nails out the decking board!'

Dangerous Dave went and got the telephone. He dialled the number of the hire company and explained that the machine was not working properly and that he needed another one.

When the men arrived, they took one look at the machine, apologised to Dangerous Dave and promised to get him another one.

Dangerous Dave was a little disappointed as he had been looking forward to getting the pink paint off the decking and painting it back to its nice red-brown colour again.

He didn't have to wait long though. Just a few days later,

the hire company called again to say that they had a new industrial sander that they could drop round later that morning.

'At last,' said Dangerous Dave. 'I can get the decking completed.'

It was a beautiful morning and Daphne and Will had gone out shopping. Sarah was staying at home as she didn't feel well, so she was curled up on the sofa in the living room, watching the television.

Dangerous Dave was outside, eagerly awaiting the arrival of the sander. When it arrived, it was even bigger and stronger than the last one. Dangerous Dave was convinced that this time the job would be even quicker and he thanked the men for bringing it round.

'We'll collect it later this afternoon,' they said. 'You won't have any problems with this one.'

Dangerous Dave plugged the machine in. He put the cable over his shoulders and pressed the 'start' button. Sarah watched with interest from the sofa to see how Dangerous Dave would get on with the new machine.

What happened next made Sarah laugh and laugh and laugh. It was the funniest thing she had ever seen.

The machine started and the power of the conveyor belt

launched the big, heavy machine forward at a tremendous speed. Dangerous Dave, who hadn't been expecting such power, was suddenly whisked off his feet and was holding onto the handlebars at the back for dear life; whilst his feet resembled those of a cartoon character, desperately whizzing and trying to stop himself from moving.

Dangerous Dave pulled hard on the handlebars. The machine turned round and Dangerous Dave went whizzing past the living room window in the direction of the garage and the side wall.

Sarah got up and walked to the living room to watch what was happening. Dangerous Dave's feet were still flying behind him; his arms desperately trying to turn the machine round.

A few seconds later, the machine followed by Dangerous Dave clinging on was whizzing past the living room window in the opposite direction and straight towards Dougie's fence!

Sarah could imagine the machine and Dangerous Dave crashing straight through the fence, leaving that man outline on the fence, before going through the garden of number 5 and through the next fence to number 4; the next fence to number 3 and so on until he came into the woods and crashed into a tree or something.

Dangerous Dave swung the machine round just narrowly avoiding going through Dougie's fence and shot past in the other direction.

There was a moment of chaos and then suddenly everything went quiet. Dangerous Dave had stumbled upon the 'off' button and hit it hard with his hand.

He appeared at the living room patio door.

'Sarah,' he puffed, his face all red and sweaty, 'I think there's something wrong with this machine!'

Sarah laughed. 'Look, dad,' she said. 'You've put a white strip all the way across the decking. Now it's pink with a white stripe.'

'I'm not talking about it,' said Dangerous Dave and he promptly went to collect the telephone to call the hire company again.

The men from the hire company arrived later that day to collect the machine. When they saw the white stripe, they smirked but tried to not laugh out loud in case they upset Dangerous Dave.

'Well,' said Dangerous Dave, when the men had gone. 'I'm never using a machine again.'

When Daphne and Will got home, Sarah told them about the fun

Dangerous Dave had been having with the machine. They came to look at the white stripe. They could only imagine what had happened and wished that there had been a video recording of the whole event.

'We would have won a prize on 'You've Been Framed'' said Will.

'Still, never mind' said Daphne. 'There's always another time.'

'Oh no, there's not,' said Dangerous Dave. 'Next year we're moving! And this time, there's going to be no more decking!'

'Okay,' said Daphne, quite pleased, that finally the decking was going to go.

Dangerous Dave smiled as he thought of what life would be like without the decking. I think he was secretly quite pleased to never have to paint the decking again!

All work is copyright and names have been deliberately changed to protect the privacy of the individuals concerned.

Printed in Great Britain
by Amazon